The Bogwater Witches

Kathy Still lives in Putney with her husband Chris and her daughters, Becky and Jessica. For the last ten years she has spent much of her time designing patterns for a major ceramics company. Before that she trained in natural history illustration at the Royal College of Art, and designed greetings cards and gift and novelty books. Her first storybook for children was *The Tractor Princess* (Orchard Books).

The Bogwater Witches

Kathy Still

Illustrated by Merida Woodford

Dolphin Paperbacks

First published in Great Britain in 1998
as a Dolphin paperback
by Orion Children's Books
a division of the Orion Publishing Group Ltd
Orion House
5 Upper St Martin's Lane
London WC2H 9EA

This edition published 2006 for Index Books Limited

A catalogue record for this book is available
from the British Library

Typeset by Deltatype Ltd, Birkenhead, Merseyside
Printed and bound in Great Britain by Clays Ltd, St Ives plc

ISBN 1 85881 579 7

For Becky and Jessica
K.S.

For children everywhere who are
made to write poems ~ H.W.

CONTENTS

Map   vi
Gazeteer   viii

1) The New Arrival   1
2) The Sign   11
3) The Celebration   21
4) The Midsummer Fair   32
5) The Mop   43
6) The Sunny Spell   53
7) The Cat   62
8) The Proficiency Test   72
9) Enter Macbeth   83
10) Moving Day   96

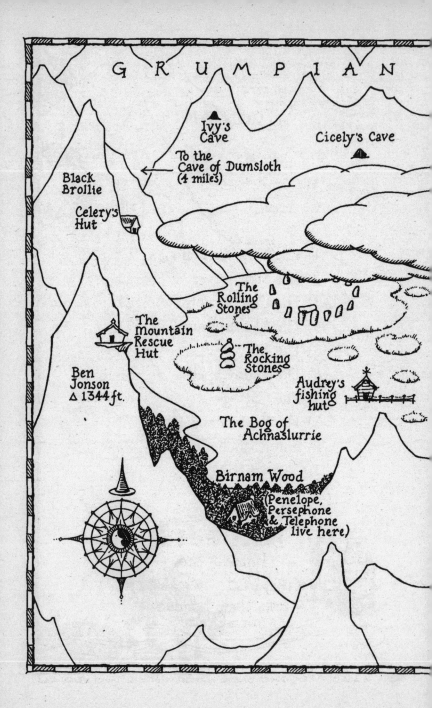

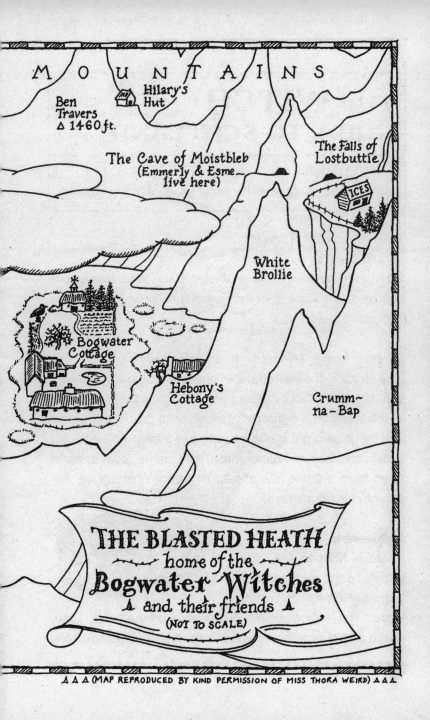

MOUNTAINS

Ben
Travers
△ 1460 ft.

Hilary's
Hut

The Cave of Moistbleb
(Emmerly & Esme
live here)

The Falls of
Lostbuttie

ICES

White
Brollie

Bogwater
Cottage

Hebony's
Cottage

Crumm~
na~Bap

THE BLASTED HEATH
~~ home of the ~~
Bogwater Witches
▲ and their friends ▲
(NOT TO SCALE)

▲ ▲ ▲ (MAP REPRODUCED BY KIND PERMISSION OF MISS THORA WEIRD) ▲ ▲ ▲

THE **WITCH**
GUIDE TO SCOTLAND

KEY TO SYMBOLS

🧹 of interest 🧹🧹 worth the detour 🧹🧹🧹 not to be missed

THE BLASTED HEATH

Population: 13.

Facilities: none, but you may shelter in the Mountain Rescue Hut (near the summit of Ben Jonson) from which there are impressive views.

Despite being featured in a well-known play by Mr Shakespeare, the Blasted Heath remains Scotland's best-kept secret. Surrounded by mountains and shrouded in mist, this desolate region is completely hidden from the outside world. Strictly speaking, it is not a heath, but a bog, whose murky waters are deep and dangerous. There are no roads or paths apart from a single row of stepping-stones (which are slippery and lead nowhere).

Sightseeing

There is little to see, due mainly to the mist, but this generally clears after mid- night. The only building (Bogwater Cottage, circa 1560) stands on the largest of several islands. It is of no architectural interest. However, there are several *caves* 🦅 in the mountainside which are well worth a visit. (Please knock before entering, as some are inhabited.) South-west of the Heath is *Birnam Wood,* 🧙 🧙 legendary birthplace of Skusting and Spatula, the so-called 'Stinking Imps'. Travelling north, we come to the *Rolling Stones* 🧙 🧙 🧙 (admission free). This fine example of a prehistoric stone circle has a total of fifteen massive stones, and is the site of the Beltane Ball and the Midsummer Fair, both of which attract many visitors. *(see festivals)*

Getting There

Access is impossible without a broomstick, and *only* experienced travellers should attempt the journey. Flying conditions can be hazardous as the weather is *extraordinarily* bad, even in summer. *n.b.* For your own safety, do not dismount unless you are absolutely sure the ground is firm. The authors cannot be held responsible for disappearances.

What to Bring Back

The Blasted Heath is the last known habitat of the marsh haddock, a local delicacy (available from Audrey's Fishing Hut).

The
Bogwater
Witches

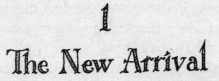

1
The New Arrival

It was a wet night in early November and Thora Weird – Chairwoman of the local Witches' Institute – sat in the parlour at Bogwater Cottage, writing her thank-you letters. Hallowe'en was a waste of time, she thought sourly. A silly fuss about nothing-in-particular, with all those wretched paper hats and appalling games, followed by days and days of leftover pumpkin, which always gave her indigestion. She hiccupped loudly at the thought of it, then dipped her pen in the ink and scrawled 'Dear Penelope, Thank you very much for…' and stopped. Did Penelope give her the crystallized newts, or was it the leech barometer? Outside the wind whined and whistled, rattling at the windows and tugging at the thatch. A sudden gust made the sausages swing

1

on their hooks in the rafters, sending down a shower of dust and sooty black drips. One landed right in the middle of Thora's letter.

'Out, damp spot!' the witch muttered crossly, rubbing in vain at the dirty mark. She was too tired to begin again, so she blew out her candle and went to warm her hands in front of the fire beside her sister Sibyl.

The Weird Sisters could hardly have been more different. Everybody loved nice old Sibyl, even though she was a bit silly. She was scared of everything, especially flying, which made her dreadfully broom-sick on the shortest journey. She looked after the animals and did all the work while Thora fiddled about in her workshop at the end of the garden.

Thora was tremendously fierce and horribly bossy, a Cauldron Bleu and Grand Librarian of the Alphabetical Order (she was the only member, no one else was allowed to join). It was said she could make a storm in a teacup, and she rode her broom-stick side-saddle, just to show off.

Sibyl was contentedly plucking ravens. 'He loves me…He loves me not…He loves me…He loves me not…' she whispered softly as she dropped the feathers into a pillowcase.

'Superstitious nonsense!' said Thora irritably, and clicked her tongue in disapproval. Then she glanced at the hourglass and saw that it was exactly ten o'clock: time for the News.

Thora lifted the crystal ball down from the mantelshelf and gazed into it. After a moment the mist cleared and she settled down to watch the pictures. Nothing unusual was going to happen (it never did). There would be a missing cat and a midair collision, a ghost had stolen a toasting-fork, and a skeleton was wanted for questioning. Apart from that, the butter would taste of garlic, and someone had spotted the Gormless Monster. Thora wasn't really paying much attention when she caught a glimpse of two familiar figures.

'It's us!' she shrieked. 'Look, Sybil! In the crystal! There's me, and you…but what's that funny pink creature?'

Sybil screwed up her eyes and peered over her sister's shoulder. 'I think it must be one of the piglets,' she said uncertainly. The picture was very poor and fading fast, so Thora gave the crystal a hefty thump with her fist. At once the old woman who foretold the weather came into view waving her piece of seaweed.

'You shouldn't be allowed!' screeched Thora, hurling the crystal across the room. It narrowly missed a chicken who was laying an egg in Sybil's knitting basket.

Thora sat and pondered on what she had seen. What had a piglet to do with anything? Could it fly? Was it bewitched? It really was too bad, the way the picture had faded like that. She would write and complain first thing tomorrow morning. Sybil finished doing the ravens and began to fidget. She glanced nervously at her sister several times before daring to ask.

'Do you hear a noise, dear?'

'Don't start that again!' snapped Thora, for her sister was always hearing things. 'Every night you ask me, and every night I tell you, *there's nothing out there!* It's just the wind.'

'I definitely heard something this time,' protested Sibyl. 'Listen!'

'And which noise am I supposed to hear tonight?' asked Thora sarcastically. 'The Wolf? The Phantom Piper? The Roman Legion?'

'None of those,' said Sibyl unhappily. 'I've not heard this one before.'

Thora stood up and stabbed at the fire with the poker. 'Any minute now you'll be telling me you can smell marsh gas,' she said irritably. 'To think…'

'There it is again!' interrupted Sibyl. 'You *must* have heard it that time! Do take a look outside, dear. I'd go myself, but you know how I hate the dark.'

'Anything for a moment's peace!' snorted her sister, flinging the door open. She glanced furiously to the left, then glared to the right, took one pace forward and nearly fell over something that was lying on the doorstep.

'What idiot left that there?' she bellowed, poking the Something with her boot. It wiggled and grunted. After a moment's hesitation Thora picked it up and dumped it in her sister's lap.

'You deal with it,' she said gruffly. 'I'm not expecting anything.'

Sybil examined the bundle cautiously. 'I'm afraid it's broken, whatever it is,' she said. 'Look, it's leaked all over me!' She untied the string, expecting to find a donation for the Witches' Institute bring-and-buy sale, but instead there was a baby with a grubby bottle and a quiff of red hair that stood up like a question mark.

'So that's what we saw in the crystal! Look, dear, it wasn't a piglet after all!' she said, holding it up for her sister to see.

'The downright cheek of some people!' spluttered Thora. 'Leaving babies lying around where respectable citizens might fall over them. I could have been seriously injured, I...'

Sybil wasn't listening. She was doing 'Round and Round the Cauldron' on the baby's chubby hand, and trying to remember how you folded a nappy. She had cared for all kinds of orphans and invalids from an albino bat to a balding badger, but never a baby!

'We must return this infant to its rightful owner as soon as possible,' said Thora. 'I shall put a notice in

my next Newsletter. Somebody must know who it belongs to.'

'But I want to keep it!' whined Sibyl. 'I'll look after it, I promise. It won't be any bother.'

'Babies are always a bother,' said Thora. 'And then there's the cost. Think how much it will eat when it's older! Now stop snivelling and hand me that empty bottle. The creature must be starving.'

Thora unscrewed the top of the baby's bottle and was just about to pour in some milk when she noticed there was a scrap of paper inside. (The child's mother was remarkably careless!) She unrolled it and found a message.

Please look after Baby. She's the last straw, what with the three sets of twins to cope with already. I've no more nappies, and no-one to turn to. My hubby has a bad back, and all of my six big brothers and sisters have gone to live in Kettering. I know this is a wicked thing to do, and I promise not to do it again.

P.S. This is how you fold a nappy.

'A likely story!' snorted Thora, prodding the baby with a bony finger. 'Nasty, smelly thing! Ugh!' She shuddered and passed the note to Sybil (who wasn't as clever as her sister, and had to hold it up to the mirror). She was puzzling over the diagrams when Thora snatched it back. After reading the message again, she gave a triumphant shriek, then swept the baby up in her arms and rocked it violently.

'Rock-a-bye Baybeeeeee on the treeeeee top,' she croaked, wiggling her ears in time to the tune. The baby grinned and was sick, but Thora didn't seem to mind at all. She thrust the baby back at Sibyl, mopped up the mess with the tea towel, and began to frolic about the room cackling with laughter. She was an unusually large lady and in stooping to avoid a low beam she tripped over a chicken and banged her head on the spinning wheel. But instead of losing her temper she just lay on the floor and laughed.

'Are you all right, dear?' enquired Sibyl. 'You don't seem quite yourself this evening.'

''Course I am! Do I look ill?'

'No dear, but you can't abide babies. You said yourself, not five minutes ago...'

'That was five minutes ago,' said Thora impatiently. 'Read this.'

'I have done,' replied Sybil. 'But I don't see...'

'Pay attention and I shall explain,' said Thora. 'According to the message this scrawny specimen is the Seventh Child of a Seventh Child. That means she'll have more power in her little finger than the

whole of the Witches' Institute put together. We've got a Giftwitch!'

'A Giftwitch?' echoed Sibyl. 'You mean...like Young Telephone*?'

Thora nodded and they stared at one another, hardly daring to believe their luck. Baby Telephone had been found at a crossroads on the other side of the mountains in a tall red box with her name on. She was now twenty-six, extremely magical, and no end of help to Penelope and Persephone, the witches who had brought her up. Sybil looked thoughtful.

* *Pronounced like Penelope*

'It could be a trick to persuade us to keep her – not that I wouldn't if she wasn't, if you see what I mean,' she added hastily.

'We must await a Sign,' said Thora in the mysterious voice she usually kept for visitors. 'And if nothing Peculiar takes place within forty-nine days the child will have to go.'

'And if Something Peculiar does happen?' asked Sybil eagerly.

'Then we keep her, you silly old nit!' retorted her sister.

Sybil beamed and crossed her eyes for luck. Then she had to uncross them to change the baby's nappy. When that was done she gave her a kiss and tucked her up in the sock-drawer, between the balding badger and a weasel with a wooden leg.

2
The Sign

Sibyl was sound asleep at six o'clock when Thora got up to gather the dew. Other witches were lazy and did their spells with spring water, but Thora was old-fashioned and insisted on doing everything properly. She bustled about the garden, stopping to tap a leaf here, a branch there, until drip by drop her jug was full. Then she popped a caterpillar in her mouth and sucked it slowly as she strolled down the path to her workshop. It was an extraordinary morning, with no wind or rain, and not a trace of mist, but Thora hardly noticed. She was thinking about her experiment.

Thora couldn't be bothered with curing warts or mixing potions; she left that sort of thing to Sibyl. She was a Scientist, an Astronomer, a Weather-

11

Changer, a Mathematician, and a Maker of Fireworks, she told people modestly. Every day she spent hours in her workshop, tipping tubes of this into tubes of that, setting fire to things and getting generally hot and bothered. Although she would never admit it, she hadn't actually discovered anything, unless you counted a cure for hiccups and a potion for getting scrambled eggs off cauldrons (and both had been accidental).

Deep in thought Thora unlocked the door, then fed the shelf and dusted the cat before settling down to work. But for some reason, she just couldn't concentrate. She muddled up the words of her Start-of-Day spell, dropped earwax into the cauldron instead of earwigs, spilled the dew, smashed a cup and slipped up in some ferret-fat. She felt so miserable that she decided to treat herself to her Special spell, the one that worked every time. Immediately the sky went dark and the weather started up again.

She soon felt happier, and happier still when she remembered the Giftwitch. If she really was the Seventh Child of a Seventh Child, there would be no end to the things they could conjure up between them. She cheered up at the thought of a well full of whisky, a comfy bed, and a shiny golden egg every morning. Of course the Giftwitch would have a great deal to learn before they could attempt anything so complicated. Her mother had been wise to bring her to Bogwater Cottage; who else could teach her the mysteries of the earth and the meaning of the universe? The lucky child would be keen to learn and eager to follow in her footsteps. And in years to come she, too, would be a Cauldron Bleu, and Chairwoman of the Witches' Institute…and perhaps even President of the Hexagon Council.

Back in the cottage Sybil awoke with a start. There was a dreadful howling and yowling and at first she thought it was the cats. Then she realized it was coming from the Giftwitch. She took a swig of tea from her hot-water bottle, splashed some more on her face, then went over to look in the sock-drawer.

'WAAAAAAA! WAAAAAA! WAAAAAAAAAA!' screamed the baby, shaking its fists in fury.

When the Giftwitch had been fed and changed Sybil put her back to bed and set about making the breakfast. There wasn't any bread left, so she seized a piglet by the scruff of the neck and popped him in the cauldron. Then she added another peat to the fire and blew on it to get it going.

'There's a good little piggy-wig!' She smiled as he snuffled about licking up the scraps of yesterday's stew. When the cauldron was nice and clean Sybil lifted him out and tipped in a mugful of oatmeal.

As she was stirring the porridge she heard a famil-iar cough from out in the yard, and after a great deal of wheezing a tattered ghost seeped through the wall. Instead of being white and wispy he was tartan, and fringed at the edges like a picnic rug. He had a funny smell too, a mixture of dirty dishcloths

13

and stale shortbread. Sybil advanced towards him waving the porridge spoon.

'And what time do you call this?' she demanded. 'I've done half your chores already.'

The ghost hung his head and started to cough, hoping Sibyl would feel sorry for him.

The witch sighed. Auld Frowstie was every bit as grumpy and grubby as when she'd found him mixed up with the second-hand cloaks at a jumble sale. He had promised that if she bought him he would help about the house, but he had turned out to be a damp, lazy creature, who complained about everything and rarely got up before midnight.

'I've a good mind to tell Thora this time,' said Sibyl, banging the kettle down noisily. At once the Giftwitch awoke and began to cry.

'Whaaaaaasssat?' shrieked the ghost, oozing back through the wall in fright.

'Don't be silly, it's only a baby,' smiled Sibyl. 'Come and see.'

'It's disgusting!' said Auld Frowstie, glaring at it. 'When's it going?'

And when Sibyl told him it might be staying, he flew into a rage and began throwing cups and plates and cooking pots all round the room. From then on he was a real nuisance and did everything he could think of to upset the Giftwitch: he pulled her hair when she was asleep, he sang rude songs, and wafted up to the rafters with her toys and bottles. Worst of all, he sometimes shut the sock-drawer when she was still inside it. When the baby howled he howled louder, and when the witches scolded him he wailed.

'Yoooooooooooo don't like meeeeeeeeeee any mooooooooore.'

'He's jealous, that's what it is,' said Sibyl and slipped him a biscuit when her sister wasn't looking. But Auld Frowstie refused to take it. What he wanted was a bottle, the same as the baby's. When Sibyl finally found one for him he complained the baby's was bigger, and didn't have a scratch. At four hundred and ninety-three he was old enough to know better, the witch thought crossly.

Six weeks passed and Thora was growing impatient. When she wasn't pacing up and down the cottage she was drumming her fingers on the kitchen table, or doing complicated calculations on the calendar. Poor Sibyl was sick with worry. She adored the Giftwitch and couldn't bear the thought of losing her. She peered into the sock-drawer a hundred times a day, hoping to see something, anything, just the teeniest bit unusual. At Penelope's suggestion she went on the Good Luck Diet, but for seven days you could only eat clover and ladybirds and after two Sybil felt so weak she had to give up. In desperation she fed the Giftwitch pumpkin soup on a silver spoon. She tickled her toes with frogs and toads and dipped her dummy in the morning dew. But the child showed no sign of being anything other than an ordinary, everyday, common-or-garden sort of baby. Occasionally she smiled, but more often than not she just rolled over and went back to sleep. It was most disturbing.

On the forty-seventh day the witches were in the kitchen having lunch. The baby sat on Sibyl's knee, staring at an owl in the rafters.

'Greedy Auntie Thora wants more din-dins,' cooed Sibyl, helping her sister to a seventh bowl of broth.

'Shut up and pass the sulphur,' growled Thora.

Sibyl smiled understandingly. Her sister was always in a bad mood at full moon. She turned her attention to the baby, who was still gazing at the owl.

'Dicky-bird!' said Sibyl. 'Big dicky-bird's having a lickle bye-byes, isn't he? Sibyl and Baby love the nice dicky-bird, don't they?'

Thora couldn't stand it any longer. She banged her spoon down on the table and roared.

'The child must go! She's been here nearly seven weeks and absolutely nothing…'

Splat! The owl landed with a squawk in the middle of her dish. He blinked at Thora and she scowled back.

'*Get out of my dinner at once!*' she bellowed, as the poor bird struggled to do just that. He hopped into a corner and began pecking little bits of swede and turnip from his feathers.

'Wretched creature!' muttered Thora. 'It's high time we ate him.'

'It wasn't his fault,' protested Sibyl.

'Well whose fault was it then?' demanded Thora.

Sybil smiled nervously. 'I think the Giftwitch did it,' she replied.

They both turned to the baby, who was sucking her thumb loudly, looking very pleased with herself.

'For once, I do believe you may be right,' said Thora, and Sibyl blushed. Fancy her sister saying that!

Once the baby had learned her trick she did it again and again. Each time the owl fell in the soup

dish she squealed and clapped her hands in delight, while Thora leaned back in her chair and roared with laughter. Eventually Sibyl carried the poor bird into the bedroom and locked the door.

'Now that we're going to keep her, we must give her a name,' she said to Thora. 'We can't keep calling her the Giftwitch. It sounds unfriendly.'

'I intend to call her Thora,' said her sister.

'That would confuse me dreadfully,' replied Sibyl. 'Aren't there any other names you like, dear?'

'No,' said Thora. 'One name sounds much the same as another to me. You choose.'

That was easier said than done. Sybil found it hard to make up her mind about anything, whether it was what to wear for the Beltane Ball or what to cook for supper on Saturday. Shall I or shan't I? Kippers or custard? There was only one way to decide such things, and that was gyromancy.

She fetched a sheet of paper and tore it into squares. On the first she wrote Myrtle, on the next Mabel, followed by Maeve and then Maureen. After that she added some nice names she had come across in Thora's encyclopaedia: Armenia, Lobelia, Crustacea and Syllabub. There was one piece of paper left and after a moment's thought she wrote Hecate. That done, she went into the garden and arranged the names in a circle, weighting each one with a stone. Then she stood in the middle, took a deep breath, and whirled round and round until she was so giddy she toppled over and her hat fell off.

19

When her head had stopped spinning Sibyl picked herself up and looked to see where her hat was pointing. Sometimes it fell exactly between two pieces of paper, making it difficult to tell what the answer was, but this time there could be no doubt. The Giftwitch was called Hecate: Hecate Weird of the Blasted Heath. It was a lovely name but much too long for such a small baby. They'd have to call her Hetty.

3

The Celebration

In the days that followed what became known as the Owl Incident, the witches began to notice all kinds of unusual things. The candles burned more brightly, the knives were always sharp, and all the eggs had double yolks. Objects tended to float around the room and often turned up in the oddest places. There were sausages on the spinning wheel and knickers in the cat basket, and the spoons disappeared altogether. Sybil's moon-mirror went missing for a whole week. Eventually she found it on the highest shelf, tucked between two of Thora's spell books.

'You *are* a little monkey,' said the witch fondly, showing the baby her reflection. Hetty gazed at herself, fascinated, then smiled shyly. The baby in the mirror pulled a rude face.

'It's all very mysterious,' said Sibyl when she told Thora that evening, 'but it would be nice if she could do something useful, like getting the fire to light.'

'That's where education comes in,' said Thora grandly. 'By the time I've finished with her she'll be a lady Merlin, you mark my words.'

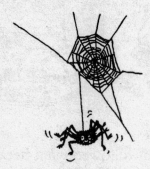

Sibyl could never remember a time when there had been so many visitors. A few ladies called in as usual to buy jars of honey and herbal ointment, but most had come to see Hetty. Since her arrival there always seemed to be a witch on the doorstep, wanting to borrow a sock cube or return a cup of sulphur.

'She's a fine baby. Are you planning to celebrate?' they would ask eagerly, hoping there was going to be a party. Sibyl suggested it to Thora and was most surprised when she agreed.

'I was thinking exactly the same thing myself,' she replied, for she was immensely proud to own a baby that could make owls fall into soup and wanted to show her off.

After some argument about the guest-list the witches decided to invite everyone, from the Wise Woman of Dumsloth to the Hag of Blackbrollie. Thora wrote fifty-three invitations in her spiky spidery lettering. Auld Frowstie was far from pleased, as it was his job to deliver them.

The
WEIRD
SISTERS
are delighted
to announce the
GIFT of a WITCH
(Hecate Thora Weird)
You are invited to a
CELEBRATION
at
Bogwater Cottage, the Blasted Heath
Next Tuesday at twelve noon sharp
your presents will be welcome ▲ R.S.V.P.*

* Return spook very promptly

23

There was much to be done. Thora drew up an elaborate menu (which she handed over to Sibyl) before settling down to write a speech. When Auld Frowstie returned he was sent to help in the kitchen, but he did nothing apart from peeling a few toadstools, which he complained had given him arm-ache. He watched poor Sibyl as she brewed and stewed and bottled and stuffed without a stop. By the end of the week she was so exhausted that she flopped on to the hearthrug beside the cats. Thora stared at her over the rim of her spectacles.

'You'll never get things done at this rate,' she said disapprovingly, and went back to rehearsing her speech.

Very early on the morning of the party, Sibyl had a shock. 'Coo-ee! We're here!' called Audrey, the witch who delivered the fish on Fridays.

'Go away! I'm not dressed yet!' shouted Sibyl.

'We've come to help,' said Audrey. The door opened and in they marched, the ladies of the

Blasted Heath Witches' Institute: Audrey, Ivy, Emmerly, Esmé, Cicely, Celery, Hilary, Hebony, Penelope, Persephone and Young Telephone. They shooed out the animals and began setting out rows of teacups straightaway. When that was done they arranged dainty jars of hemlock and deadly night-shade on the windowsills. Young Telephone put up signs on the outhouses that said 'Cloakroom', 'Cat Room' and 'Parking for 50 Broomsticks'. While the other ladies were making vole-aux-vents and stuffing toadstools, Sibyl gave Hetty a bath in the water-bucket. Then she brushed her hair and dressed her in a nightie with little red earwigs embroidered on the collar. After flicking away a final cobweb she hurried out to greet her guests.

Thora was already in the yard. She looked very smart in her Black Witch tartan cloak and hat. Round her neck she wore a gallstone necklace and in either hand she held a bat to beckon the visitors in to land. As soon as the first witch drew near Thora began waving her arms about wildly, bellowing instructions at the top of her voice. The poor lady was so alarmed she lost her nerve entirely and landed upside down in the newt-pond.

Soon Bogwater Cottage was crammed with witches, all cackling and gossiping and bumping into one another. 'It can't be...I don't believe it...it is!' they cried. 'Why, I haven't seen you for Hallowe'ens!' It became so crowded that some sprightly ladies climbed up into the rafters, where

25

they sat playing tunes on combs and paper. Others
settled down on the floor, knitting little black
bonnets and taking it in turns to bounce Hetty
about on their knees. She didn't seem to mind, and
gurgled with delight when it was time to open her
presents. There were the usual cuddly slugs and
woolly weasels, but the one Hetty liked best was a
wooden rattle, carved by a white-haired lady from
Achnaslurrie.

'It does make a good noise!' exclaimed Sibyl.
'What did you put inside, dear?'

'Teeth,' she replied proudly. 'Some were mine, the
rest belonged to Puss.'

The guests hadn't only brought presents for Hetty,

they also had something to give Sibyl and that was Advice. She learned that a baby's clothes should be worn back-to-front (for safety) and inside-out (for warmth), that you must *never* wash behind their ears (it makes them deaf) and *on no account* should you add sulphur to their supper till they're six months old. Poor Sibyl was horribly confused. She hadn't realized that looking after a baby could be so complicated. To her relief the cauldron began to boil over, giving her an excuse to slip away.

The witches were still arguing over baby-changing spells when the food was served. While Sybil poured cups of nettle tea and dandelion coffee, Auld Frowstie hovered about with dishes of delicious cakes and home-made gobbles.

'The grreeeeeeeeen ones are cheeeeeeeeese and bunion, the bloooooooo ones are rum 'n' raven, and the grey ones are smoked maggot,' he droned.

'Very toothsome,' said the witches, greedily eyeing the venom meringue pie (which Sibyl was saving for teatime).

When they had eaten, the witches were eager to see Hetty do her trick.

'We haven't had my speech yet,' objected Thora, but nobody seemed to hear so she said it again.

'Do let's have a demonstration,' begged a lady called Edwina. 'I've flown forty miles to see her.'

'And it's my birthday today,' piped up an old lady in the rafters. 'I'm eighty-five.'

'We haven't had my speech yet,' shouted Thora and

when someone suggested they watched the trick instead she ripped up her script and stormed into the bedroom, slamming the door behind her. Sybil was wondering whether to go after her when she reappeared clutching Owl, who looked almost as irritable as she did. When Hetty caught sight of him she beamed and made a funny noise. Everyone laughed.

'She always does that when she sees him,' said Thora fondly, forgetting she was supposed to be in a temper.

There was silence as everyone glanced up at Owl, then down to Hetty and back again. Nothing happened.

'Let's give it a few more minutes,' suggested Sybil brightly. 'She's probably rather shy about doing it in front of other people.'

Suddenly there was a flash of lightning followed by a crack of thunder that shook the tiny cottage. The door burst open to reveal three ragged witches standing arm-in-arm, their cloaks flapping in the wind. Somebody gasped but no one said a word. The newcomers grinned and nudged one another.

'What's the matter – cats got yer tongues?' shrieked one and they all hooted with laughter.

'Long time, no see!' spluttered another.

'Remember us?' shrilled the third.

How could anyone ever forget these scheming, sneering, sniggering sisters? Rubella, Smerelda and Firkettle were quite unlike other witches. They swaggered and swore and scratched and spat. They hated everyone and spoiled everything with their spiteful spells and bad behaviour. It was twenty years since they had been banned from the Witches'

Institute for receiving stolen broomsticks and being cruel to cats. In a fit of rage they had put a curse on the Blasted Heath. For seven years the porridge never thickened and the pumpkins shrivelled, the animals sickened and the stars went dim. Everyone was thoroughly miserable. Then one night the curse was lifted and the witches disappeared in an eclipse of the moon. No one knew where they had gone or what had become of them, and nobody had cared to find out.

'Well? Aren't you going to ask us in?' demanded Rubella and barged straight in, followed by Smerelda and Firkettle.

'Well, pickle my knickers, it's quite a party!' she sneered. She walked slowly round the room, staring at each frightened witch in turn. Her eyes fell on the cakes, the gobbles and the plates of buns, then she spat in the sugar and helped herself to a piece of black pudding.

'Shame they forgot to invite us, eh, Firkettle?' she mumbled with her mouth full and

Firkettle burped loudly in agreement.

'Slipped your mind, did it, Weird?' shrilled Smerelda.

'What do you want?' asked Thora, her voice little more than a whisper.

'Come to see the baby, haven't we, ducky?' said Rubella, making a beeline for Hetty who was propped up in the sock-drawer.

'Ugly little boggart, isn't she?' cackled Smerelda, giving her a hard pinch. 'Say "Hello" to your aunties, dearie.'

Hetty began to cry and suddenly the three intruders whipped out their wands and waved them over her.

'If this precious kiddie is ever stung by a nettle...' snarled Rubella, pausing to catch a fly on the end of her tongue.

'We'll cut off her power!' they all shrieked at once. And with that (and the venom meringue pie) they left.

4
The Midsummer Fair

Kind, wispy Sibyl was a green witch. She understood the earth and things that grew and did most of her gardening at midnight, whatever the weather. It had something to do with the moon (but nobody was quite sure what, because Sybil wasn't very good at explaining). She loved her plants and couldn't pull up a turnip without getting upset. 'I'm terribly sorry,' she would apologize. 'This is going to hurt me far more than it hurts you.' So when it came to burning her nettle patch she burst into floods of tears and Thora had to do it for her.

'Better safe than sorry,' she grunted, stamping on the embers in her hobnail boots.

'What a waste!' sighed Sibyl. 'Nettles are so useful. And they make such lovely soup.'

She waited until her sister was out of sight, then fell to her knees and examined every speck of earth to make absolutely sure there was nothing left that could harm dear Hetty.

Sybil had already found that looking after a baby, as well as six cats, five piglets, two goats, a ghost and a sister, was rather harder than she had expected and it was harder still when the baby learned to crawl. Hetty seemed to attract knives and nails and got hold of the kitchen scissors so often that Sybil was mystified, until one day quite by accident she discovered Hetty was magnetic. She was electric too, when a storm was in the air. Her red hair sparked and crackled and Sybil sometimes got a nasty shock when she went to pick her up.

'I don't know whether I'm coming or going these days,' she complained to Audrey, when she called in one Friday to deliver the fish.

'They're into everything at that age, aren't they?' said her friend sympathetically, moving an axe out of Hetty's reach. The Giftwitch gave an angry squawk and crawled behind the peat basket.

'What you need is a spell,' said Audrey. 'If you can spare five minutes and a piece of chalk, I'll show you my granny's old trick.'

Granny's old trick was remarkably easy. You just drew a circle round the baby, tapped it with a wand, and commanded it to stay. In a flash you had an escape-proof playpen. 'What goes in, can't get out,' Audrey explained. 'It takes a bit of getting used to, what with it being invisible. You can make it any size you like. When you want to let her out, just rub away a bit of the circle and write EXIT there instead. Hey presto! Spell's broken and Baby's on the loose again! Now let's see you do it.'

Sibyl got it right first time. She had been afraid Hetty wouldn't like being in a playpen, but it didn't seem to bother her. Whenever she reached the edge of the circle she burst out laughing, and Sibyl soon realized it wasn't just invisible, it was tickly, too.

'Clever, isn't it?' said Audrey. She gave Sybil a few more useful tips and flew off to finish her fish-round.

'All gone, Audrey!' Sibyl said.

'Bah,' replied Hetty solemnly, holding up the breadknife for her to see. Without thinking Sybil rushed into the playpen to get it back.

'Help!' she wailed. 'Frowstie! Do something!' but the ghost merely yawned and wafted up to the rafters to watch the fun.

Hetty had a way with animals as well as owls. She sat on her rug and stared at a piglet till he woke up and wandered into the playpen. He was joined by a baby weasel, a brown rat, a black cat, a goat, a goose, three chickens, six mice, a toad, a hedgehog, and two dozen snails that Sibyl had collected for lunch. The cat licked her lips when she saw the mice. In the nick of time Sibyl scooped them up in her pointed hat and held it above her head. She looked on in despair as Hetty pulled off all her clothes and put them on the piglet, while the other animals tore

round the playpen, squeaking and squawking. They were there for three whole hours (and would have been there even longer if Thora hadn't cut her finger and come in for a cobweb from the first-aid box).

As time passed the witches began to suspect there was something not-quite-right about their Hetty. With her rust-red hair and cheeky grin she didn't look like a witch at all. She didn't behave like one either. For a start she was squeamish and made a ridiculous fuss about her food. She wouldn't eat mink or rat or rook, she picked all the maggots out of her cheese, and she even turned up her nose at beans on stoat. At bedtime she brushed her teeth and took off her boots, and (to the witches' disgust)

35

she actually washed her socks. When she was six Thora caught her twirling round the garden in the kitchen curtains, pretending to be a fairy. (There was a picture of one in Sybil's gardening book, on the page headed 'Garden Pests'.) 'It's just a stage. She'll grow out of it when she's older, you'll see,' the other ladies said comfortingly but Sybil and Thora weren't convinced.

Ever since she was little Hetty's powers had been getting her into trouble. Sometimes she couldn't control them but Thora thought she was just plain naughty. 'You've more power than sense, my girl!' the witch would say, but secretly she was envious. The more she wanted Hetty to do something the more determined Hetty was not to do it. She certainly wasn't keen to be a witch. Although she liked reading her writing was shocking and came out back-to-front, just like her mother's. She played pranks and tricks and practical jokes and squabbled with Auld Frowstie till she drove Thora mad. Then the witch would lock her in the broom-cupboard and refused to let her out till she had written a poem for the W.I. Newsletter.

Hetty spent a lot of time in the broom-cupboard. She was there on the day of the Midsummer Fair, which was the jolliest day of the witches' year except for Hallowe'en. It was held at a mysterious ring of rocks called the Rolling Stones, and people flew from miles around to join in the fun. There were races and raffles, fiddlers and fortune-tellers, competitions to Guess the Weight of the Snake or How Many Beaks in the Jar. At eight o'clock there was a flying display, and at sunset the ladies lit an enormous bonfire and danced around until it was dark enough for fireworks.

Hetty was in the cupboard because she had broken the newt-dish. Or rather, Auld Frowstie had broken the newt-dish but he had melted through the wall when Thora came in, and Hetty got the blame. It wasn't fair! Thora never made him write poems, she thought miserably. She was plotting her revenge when the witch tapped sharply on the door.

'If you haven't finished in ten minutes I'm leaving you behind.'

'I want to come!' wailed Hetty. Magic was no use at all when it came to poems but that was the whole point, she supposed.

'One minute to go,' called Thora. 'Fifty seconds… forty seconds…thirty seconds…twenty seconds…'

'*Finished!*' shrieked Hetty. She slid a sheet of paper under the door and waited anxiously as the witch read what she had written.

Spider! Spider! Lurking fright
In my cupboard, late at night
When I meet your beady eye
I'm awful glad I'm not a fly!

37

'Utter piffle!' snorted Thora. Then she unlocked the door and said, 'Hurry along, spit spot! I want to take off in two minutes.'

The ladies of the Witches' Institute had been at the Rolling Stones all day, struggling to and fro with trestle tables, wobbling about on ladders, and getting into a flap over the tea-tent. Much to their relief their Chairwoman usually stayed at home until everything was ready. She would appear at about ten to six, just in time to deliver her speech, cut the ribbon and declare the fair open. This year she was a little early and the witches were still stringing up the last few lanterns when she arrived.

'Stay by me, Hecate, I don't want you getting lost,' she snapped. 'We've time for a tour of inspection before I give my speech.'

Obediently Hetty trailed after her as she wound her way through the maze of little stripy stalls selling shortcake, candles, kippers and baskets, goose-grease, rush lights, pigs, wigs, wands, whistles, and a hundred and one other useful things. As she passed the witch nodded to people and said, 'Lovely to see you!' and 'Keep up the good work!'

She stopped to adjust a sign over a sweet stall and admired a display of candied fish and fruits.

'May I have a toffee apple?' begged Hetty.

'We're not really open yet, dearie,' smiled the witch behind the counter. 'But as you've got such a nice smile, I'll give you one for free.'

Hetty beamed and stretched out her hand to take it – but Thora got there first. 'It's a kind thought, but they're bad for the child's teeth,' she said.

Next, Thora inspected the tea-tent and Hetty asked if she could have a sandwich, but the witch refused, telling her she should have eaten her omelette at lunchtime.

'But I don't like lizard's eggs,' protested Hetty. 'Sybil always lets me have chicken's ones instead.'

'Well, she shouldn't! Anyway you could have eaten the shells. You'll never have nails like mine if you don't.'

Then Hetty begged to have a drink but the witch said no, because if she did they'd be traipsing backwards and forwards to the bog all evening.

'Mean old bat!' muttered Hetty.

'I heard that, Hecate,' said Thora. 'I was going to give you some spending money (a limited amount, mind you, as I shall have to replace the newt-bowl). But as you have been so rude I have decided against it.'

It was almost time to open the fair. Thora left Hetty by the sweet stall and asked the lady to keep an eye on her. Hetty made up her mind to go and

39

look for Sibyl. Sibyl was nice, she would give her some pocket money, and a drink, and a toffee-apple, and a go on the tombola.

'And don't try sneaking off to find my sister because I shall be watching you,' said Thora sternly. 'I've got eyes in the back of my head.' With that she walked briskly up onto the stage and rapped her wand on the table for silence.

'Good evening and welcome, ladies and gentlemen, witches and wizards, to this, the three-hundred-and-thirty-seventh Midsummer Fair at the Rolling Stones…'

Thora was still speaking twenty minutes later and the crowd was growing impatient. Witches grumbled and muttered under their breath, and a rude old wizard shouted, 'Get on with it, Missus!' At that moment a row of gingerbread men rose up from a table behind the platform, formed themselves into a pyramid, and hovered in the air above Thora's hat. Then they jumped down, bowed, and clattered back onto their plate. Thora was pleased to see everyone smiling at her anecdote about the dictionary and went on to tell another. Behind her back a dozen eels wiggled along in a wavy line while a piece of rope whirled round and round like a Catherine wheel. People nudged one another and giggled. Thora began to feel uneasy.

'What's going on?' she asked suspiciously but nobody answered, and after pausing to glare at the crowd she continued. Everyone thought the show had finished until a black pudding leapt up

and hit a haggis, and when the haggis hit back the crowd burst into loud applause and Thora beamed delightedly.

She was about to cut the ribbon and declare the fair open when her hat lifted off her head, turned upside down, and spun round, right under her nose. The haggis plopped into it and then the black pudding. The audience screamed with laughter but Thora didn't find it at all funny.

'Who is responsible for this?' she demanded, but she knew there was only one person who was capable of such a thing. 'Will you come forward, please, Hecate,' she said ominously and everyone was silent as the little girl stepped up onto the stage.

'Is this your doing, child?' asked Thora.

Hetty didn't answer.

'This shocking misuse of magical power is not the sort of behaviour I expect from a witch. A witch should be dignified, helpful, respectful and respectable. *You* are a disgrace. What have you to say for yourself?'

Hetty shuffled and mumbled something.

'Speak up, child, I can't hear you,' said Thora. 'And stand up straight when I'm speaking to you!'

Hetty stood up straight, she drew a long, deep breath, and in front of everyone, from Young Telephone to the Wise Woman of Dumsloth, she yelled,

'I DON'WANNABEYAWITCH!!!'

5
The Mop

They didn't stay long at the Midsummer Fair. After Hetty's outburst Thora insisted on flying straight back to Bogwater Cottage without so much as a go on the tombola. In her fury she exceeded the speed limit, sending other witches scattering in all directions. Sybil followed, very slowly, with Hetty sulking behind her on the passenger seat. They both stared straight ahead, not daring to looking down in case they were broomsick. Sybil was upset because she was fond of Hetty and would have loved her every bit as much if she hadn't been the Seventh Child of a Seventh Child. Unlike Thora she hardly ever scolded her and would never have made her write a poem, let alone locked her in the broom-cupboard. Whenever she had a moment to spare she made Hetty kites and cakes and treacle toffee, or led her round the garden on the back of one of the goats. Audrey was kind to her too, and sometimes took her fishing for eels and marsh haddock. One night she found a long rope near the Mountain Rescue Hut and used it to make Hetty a swing in the crab-apple tree. (She was good at things like that.) At the end of the day, if Thora wasn't around, Sibyl would let Hetty gaze into the crystal for half an hour before she went to bed. 'But not a moment longer, dear, it's bad for your eyes.'

Early in the morning Hetty would fetch the water and feed the animals while Sybil pottered about the garden, gathering the herbs for her potions. Occasionally she made stain remover or coven cleaner but more often than not she made medicines. Emergency Mixture No. 1 was everybody's favourite because it tasted like boiled liver, while Emergency Mixture No. 5 could cure almost anything from a flea in the ear to a frog in the throat. It could often be smelt brewing in the kitchen at Bogwater Cottage and Hetty would usually be there too, stirring the cauldron and corking the potion bottles.

Hetty's favourite day of the week was Tuesday because that was when Sibyl made the flying ointment. It was a slimy concoction of herbs and moths and mutton fat which had to be boiled for three whole turns of the hourglass. While it was cooking Sibyl would sing to Hetty and tell her funny stories

about when she was a little girl. Later, when the potion had cooled, it was Hetty's job to press a plump bluebottle into the top of every jar.

'A fly in the ointment avoids disappointment,' she and Sybil would chant together, and then Sybil would add proudly,

'It's a symbol of quality.'

After that Hetty would put on the lids and stick on the labels, which had a picture of a winking witch and the words 'I'd never leave the ground without it.' And that was true; the most powerful broomstick was no better than an ordinary broom unless it was greased with flying ointment. There were many different kinds but everyone agreed that

Weird's Wonderful was the best. You only needed a little and a single pot would last for fifty miles. The recipe was so secret that Sibyl's granny had made her learn the list of herbs by heart, and then eat it, between two thick slices of brown bread and butter.

One Tuesday morning Hetty was perched on the kitchen dresser swinging her legs. She watched as Sibyl dipped her jug in the cauldron and scooped out the last of the hot potion. The witch was pouring it into jars, slowly and carefully, when Auld Frowstie crept up behind her.

'*Boo!*' he said loudly.

Sybil jumped, the jug slipped from her hands and smashed into pieces.

'Now look what you've made me do, you silly nincomspook!' she said crossly. 'We'll be six jars short, thanks to you.'

Auld Frowstie tittered. Hetty knelt down and began to blot up the flying ointment with a corner of her cloak.

'No, no, don't do that Hetty! Use the mop!' wailed Sybil. 'Get out of my kitchen! Be off with you!' she shouted at Auld Frowstie, and she blew him away with the bellows to show she meant it.

Hetty finished wiping up the flying ointment and carried the mop outside.

'Look, Sybil! Look at me! This is what Thora does!' she called from the doorway. She swung her leg over the mop and pulled a fierce face. Then in a deep voice she growled,

'Fair is foul, and foul is fair,
Hover through the fog and filthy air.'

Sibyl thought it was very funny. Hetty had got the voice just right, but she didn't say so.

'That's extremely rude, Hecate,' she told her. 'Put that down and come and help clear away some of these things.'

'All right,' grumbled Hetty but before she could get off there was a high-pitched whistling noise and the mop shot into the air like a rocket.

'Come back!' yelled Sybil and ran into the garden, screaming at the top of her voice, but Hetty was no more than a speck in the distance.

The row brought Thora hurrying from the workshop, shaking a test tube. 'What's going on?' she demanded.

'It's Hetty! She's up there! On the mop! She'll go over the mountain and we'll never see her again. I can feel it in my bones!'

'A mop?' echoed Thora, thinking she must have misheard. 'How on earth did that happen?'

'I don't know,' said Sibyl turning rather red.

The witches were still wondering what to do when Ivy came in to land. She stomped straight across the cabbage patch, jabbing the air with her broomstick.

'Your Hetty nearly knocked me flying! The speed she was doing! There's going to be an accident, you mark my words! I'm surprised at you, letting a kiddie her age out all by herself.'

At first Hetty had felt shocked. She hadn't expected to leave the ground at all, let alone so suddenly.
Flying always made her feel sick. She clenched her
teeth and clung to the mop, wishing to goodness she
had Sybil in front of her. Far below she could see the
witches waving their arms and shouting.

'Just wait till I get my hands on you, young lady!'
snarled Thora when the little girl reappeared.

'Hold on!' wailed Sybil. 'You'll fall!'

'I'd better go after her,' said Thora, grabbing Ivy's
broomstick.

'No need. I know a spell that should do the trick,'
said Ivy.

Sibyl couldn't bear to watch so she pulled her
cloak over her head and peeped through a hole. She
saw Ivy pull a wand from her sock and plant it in the
ground, magic end upward, like a firework. Then,
stretching her arms out wide, she cried,

> '*Witch be nimble*
> *Witch be quick*
> *Witch fly off the handlestick.*'

'What happens now?' asked Thora.

'We have to wait till she flies over the wand. That
activates the ejector seat,' replied Ivy.

'It's a mop. It hasn't got a seat,' objected Thora.

'Shouldn't make any difference,' said Ivy. 'Just be
patient.'

They saw Hetty circle the cottage backwards,

48

and then she skimmed low over the Blasted Heath, disappearing in the direction of Birnam Wood.

'There might be wolves in that wood,' said Sibyl from inside her cloak.

'Don't be so stupid!' snapped her sister, who had something far more important to worry about. She turned to Ivy and said,

'If the child falls now, she could get stung. That wood is full of nettles. Without her power she'll be useless. *Completely* useless,' she added ominously.

They were solemnly considering the dangers of the woods when they heard Hetty's voice from somewhere overhead.

'*Don't just stand there, do something!*' she screamed. The witches looked up and were just in time to see her catapulted high into the air, while the mop zig-zagged gently downwards like a falling leaf.

'*Heeeeeeelp!*' cried Hetty. 'Get me out!'

She had landed a few feet from the end of the garden and was up to her middle in slippery mud. Thora shouted 'Serves you right!' and Ivy yelled 'That'll teach you!' while Sibyl stood on a rickety rock and tugged and tugged, but poor Hetty was well and truly stuck.

'Don't just stand there laughing, come and help!' Sibyl screamed. 'She's sinking.'

Ivy held onto Thora, who held onto Sibyl, who clutched Hetty's hands, and the witches pulled together with all their might.

'Heave...ho!'

'Heave...ho!'

'Heave...ho!'

There was a disgusting sucking noise, followed by a loud plop! Hetty shot out of the mud like a cork from a bottle and the three witches toppled backwards in a heap.

'Well, I never want to do that again,' said Hetty when she was warm and dry and thoroughly scolded. 'But I bet *you* would!' she added, grinning slyly at Thora.

The witch's eyes goggled. 'Do what?' she growled.

'Fly a mop,' said Hetty. 'It's easy when you know how.'

That night Thora leafed through her learned books and encylopaedias but there was no mention of anyone who was able to fly a mop. Broomsticks, yes, and in certain cases, carpets (but they had been foreigners). Was it the mop that was magic, or was it that good-for-nothing girl? There was only one way to find out. She waited until Hetty and Sibyl were asleep, then tiptoed into the kitchen and took a jar of flying ointment from the cupboard. First she rubbed some on her ankles, then her ears, her elbows, her hat and her knees, her legs, and last of all the mop (she always got dressed in alphabetical order, too). When she was ready she went into the garden and sat on the mop in the moonlight.

'*Fair is foul, and foul is fair,*
Hover through the fog and filthy air,' she recited.

'Move, I command you!' she bellowed and stamped her foot. Suddenly she felt silly. Whatever was she doing? She had a perfectly good broomstick in the cupboard, the latest model, with an adjustable seat and a slug compartment. It was all Hecate's fault.

'It's so unfair!' she cried, shaking her fist at the moon. 'All that power, gone to waste on a slip of a thing who can't shell a cockroach without being sick! Why, oh why, did it have to be her?'

6
The Sunny Spell

Thora was a weather witch, and a very good one too. Given the ingredients, she could conjure up almost anything from a sheet of lightning to a blanket of snow. Her meddlesome spells annoyed the neighbours because they never knew what was coming next. 'That Weird woman's at it again,' they would grumble when Thora whipped up a wind to fly her kite or an August frost to make herself a lolly. Sometimes the mist was so thick that the witches were grounded and couldn't go out for days on end. They were always calling at Bogwater Cottage to complain, but Thora wouldn't apologize. 'The mist is an inevitable by-product of my experiments,' she would say, and march back into her workshop.

On special occasions the witches would take it in turns to do magic tricks. And if the weather was fine, and she had drunk a little whisky, Thora would do her party piece. People were amazed when she made the sun go in by shading her eye with an envelope but she couldn't make it come out again, no matter what she did. She had been searching for a Sunny Spell for nineteen years and was no nearer to finding the formula than the day she started. As far as she could tell no one had *ever* been able to make the sun come out. There was nothing about it in any of her books and even the Wise Woman of Dumsloth, who knew everything there was to know about weather, had shaken her head gravely and said, 'Impossible!'

Thora didn't especially like the sun. She declared it was far too bright and it made her sneeze. But she did like a challenge, and she had a very good reason for wanting to find the formula: the spell would be named after her and printed in the Witches' Almanack. When she closed her eyes Thora could even see the page with the heading 'Solaris Magus Thoraweirdii' in bold black letters, and a scratchy picture of her sitting at her desk.

One morning Persephone called at Bogwater Cottage to buy a pot of Emergency Mixture No. 5.

'I've got something for you,' she said to Hetty. 'I was turning out a cupboard in the kitchen and I found this. It used to be Telephone's when she was a little girl.'

She handed Hetty a small black sack tied up with a rumpled ribbon. Attached to it was a faded label with the words 'The Little Witch's Cauldron Set – Just Like Mother's!' Hetty rummaged about and brought out a small cauldron, a sawn-off wand, an hourglass, a mirror, a bowl, a beaker, eight small bottles and a stone with a hole in it. Hetty would much rather have had a pastry set, or a small dustpan and brush, but she thanked Persephone politely just the same. She arranged her new toys on the kitchen table and gazed at them until Sybil told her to stop daydreaming and pack them away, because it was nearly time for dinner.

'*Another* sunny morning!' remarked Sibyl in surprise a few days later. 'It's not often we get weather like this.'

Thora was reading a book about astronomy, and only half-listening.

'Mmmmmmmmm,' she grunted. A minute afterwards she leapt to her feet and rushed into the garden where Hetty was playing. She stood behind her and watched as she spooned something into her little cauldron.

'Are you doing a spell, Hecate?' she asked, hoping she didn't sound too interested.

'Yep,' replied Hetty, without looking up.

Normally Thora got very cross when Hetty said 'yep' instead of 'yes' (which was why she said it, of course), but this time she pretended not to notice.

'What have you got in your cauldron today?'

'It's a secret.'

'But you'll let *me* into your secret, won't you?' said Thora, almost bursting with excitement.

'Nope,' said Hetty, dropping in a dandelion.

After lunch Hetty was sitting on her swing singing a nursery rhyme. Thora decided to try again. She pushed Hetty for a while and then she said, 'We both know you made the sun come out this morning, don't we, sweetie? It's a good spell – a very good spell, but it's no use unless we have the formula. How do you do it, Hetty?'

When Hetty didn't reply, she shouted, 'For goodness' sake, Hecate, stop singing that ridiculous song, and answer my question!'

'What?' said Hetty.

'Just tell me what you put in your cauldron.'

'A neggy.'

Thora jotted it down in her notebook. 'What else?' she asked eagerly. Hetty thought for a long time. 'Yellow things,' she said at last. 'Can I go now? I want to see what's in the crystal.'

The next morning Thora was all ready to fly off to a meeting at the Rolling Stones when Hetty said, 'There were Actions.'

'Actions? What do you mean, actions? Explain yourself, child.'

'Actions,' repeated Hetty. 'To go with the spell.'

'Why didn't you say so before?' said Thora in exasperation.

'You didn't ask,' said Hetty.

'Just tell me what you did. Think, child, think!'

'What?' asked Hetty. It was fun annoying Thora. She got redder and redder, till her eyes boggled and she looked like a beetroot.

On her way to the Rolling Stones Thora had an idea. She made a swift about-turn and headed back to Bogwater Cottage. She dashed into the workshop and climbed up the rope ladder to the loft. The chemical cabinet was blocking the window but after much effort she managed to move it. She paused for a moment to catch her breath, then seized her telescope and focused her gaze on the garden below. There she was, the little minx, sitting on a mossy patch of grass between the new pond and the sundial. With a cunning smile Thora took an envelope from her pocket and held it over her eye. Then she said in a mysterious voice,

> '*I summon you Cirrus! And high Altocumulus!*
> *Nimbus and Stratus, obscure the sky!*
> *Come, lumbering, thundering Cumulonimbus*
> *And cover the sun as I cover my eye.*'

After that she started to count, not in English, but in an ancient language known only to witches. And when the sky was dark enough she returned to her telescope.

For the next three weeks, Thora spied on Hetty, and the sun went in and out. One morning (when it was in) Thora was busy in the garden. She was arranging things on the grass in alphabetical order: bog-water, brimstone, broombuds and buttercups, cake-crumbs, cat-food, cold fat and custard, dandelions, duck eggs, marigolds and mustard, saffron, smoked fish, soft soap, a stone with a hole in it, and last but not least a yellow duster. Quite the strangest set of ingredients she had ever seen, she thought, but there could be no doubt that it worked. After twenty-one days spent peering through her telescope she had pieced together the whole of Hetty's spell and couldn't wait to try it out. There was nothing difficult about mixing the potion, but the actions were most undignified. 'I shall suffer in the name of Science,' Thora told herself, and hoped that nobody would be flying over the cottage while she was suffering. After checking through her list she fetched her cat, adjusted her hat, and solemnly sat on an egg.

Hetty was sitting up in the crab-apple tree. Now it was her turn to spy on Thora. She giggled when Thora washed the fish. She spluttered when Thora ate the buttercups. She nearly split her sides when Thora peered through the stone with the hole in it.

And when Thora tried to turn cartwheels, she laughed so much the tree shook and a shower of tiny crab-apples tumbled onto the grass.

'Serves you right, for making me write poems!' thought Hetty as Thora patiently stirred the little cauldron, pausing every few minutes to stare at the sky. It was a murky colour, like mushroom soup.

Hetty watched and waited until Thora was so cross, she stamped on her second-best hat. Then Hetty began to sing, ever so softly,

> 'Twinkle, twankle, sunsie star,
> Howsie wowsie wotsie yar.
> Huppa bubba worlsie high,
> Liker neggie inver skigh,
> Twinkle, twankle, sunsie star,
> Howsie wowsie wotsie yar.'

Slowly the sky began to brighten, then turned to a pale blue, and shadows fell across the grass.

Thora cried 'Eureka!', grabbed her hat, and rushed indoors to tell Sibyl how clever she was.

When the witch had gone Hetty took a bottle from her pocket. She didn't need cartwheels or cauldrons to make the sun come out. It was much simpler than that! There had been seven empty bottles in the Little Witch's Cauldron set but the eighth had never been opened because Young Telephone had the wrong sort of hair. In fact, the potion was no use to anyone except for Hetty and now she was down to the very last drop. She resolved to save it for a rainy day and grinned wickedly as she re-read the label.

SUN POTION * FACTOR 13

Especially formulated for redheads. (Unsuitable for other hair-types)

Directions: Apply sparingly to tip of nose and little toe before breakfast.

Sun will appear between sunrise and sunset when you sing the magic words. (See label on reverse)

Warning. Always wear your hat when summoning the sun. Avoid charcoal.

At the bottom of the label, in tiny letters, it said, 'Limited edition. Active ingredient now extinct.' Hetty sighed. It had been fun while it lasted, and silly old Thora was still none the wiser. She decided to leave her bottle on the kitchen table and make a dash for it, before she got locked in the broom-cupboard. It would be a shame to stay in on such a lovely day!

7
The Cat

The witches had been invited for tea with Emmerly and Esmé. Hetty wanted to finish her fairy picture and was in a bad mood.

'Do I have to go?' she asked sullenly.

'Of course you do,' said Thora. 'Hurry up, or you'll make us late.'

'I hate their cave, it stinks!' said Hetty.

'That's quite enough!' scolded Thora. 'And while we're on the subject of behaviour, I want you to mind your manners while we're out. *Always* dunk your biscuits, *don't* talk unless your mouth is full, and remember to burp when you've had enough. Is that understood?'

'Yes, Thora,' said Hetty meekly, noting that Thora had forgotten to mention making rude noises when she sat down.

A number of other ladies were already at the Cave of Moistbleb when Thora and Sibyl arrived with Hetty. Emmerly took their hats and hung up their cloaks, while her sister fussed around plumping up cushions and handing round plates. 'Mind the stalactites, won't you, dears?' she clucked but the warning came too late. While the witches were cursing and rubbing their heads Hetty perched on a bench between Cicely and Celery, looking cross. The cave did smell horrible, whatever Thora said. Emmerly and Esmé bred cats, and the creatures were everywhere, prinking and preening, prowling and scowling, curled up on cushions and cupboards and mats, and sitting daintily on ledges like china ornaments.

In spite of their smelly cave Emmerly and Esmé were very refined. They didn't have powdered sulphur: theirs came in little cubes, which you dropped into your tea with a pair of pewter tongs. Everything was beautifully embroidered (even their ghost) and scented with a sprinkling of Norfolk Lavatory. There was a lacy collar on every cat and all the bats had tinkly bells.

'Does everybody have tea?' asked Esmé. 'Oh, Hetty, I nearly forgot you! I expect you'd like a cold drink.'

'Please don't go to any bother,' said Hetty quickly. 'I'll have a glass of water.'

'It's no trouble, no trouble at all!' beamed Emmerly. 'All children drink squash, that's one thing I do know!'

Hetty's heart sank as she watched Esmé take two plump slugs from the dish on the sideboard, drop them in a glass, and squash them with the end of the rolling pin. Then she poured in some water and handed the drink to Hetty.

'Packed with vitamins!' she beamed. 'And how about one of my home-made butterfly cakes to go

with it? Go on, have two! You're a Growing Girl!'

'Thank you very much,' said Hetty weakly, taking the only one without a butterfly.

After tea Esmé said, 'We've got a little surprise for Hetty, haven't we, Emmerly?'

'We have indeed,' said her sister. She struggled forward with an enormous basket and placed it on the floor in front of Hetty.

'Choose a kitten,' smiled Emmerly. 'Take your time, there's no hurry.'

'I don't want a cat,' said Hetty. 'I want a dog.'

These were shocking words to say in front of witches, especially when they had been kind enough to invite you to tea. Thora was deeply embarrassed.

'Don't be silly, Hecate. You don't know what you're talking about. You've never even seen a dog,' she said crossly.

'Yes, I have!' retorted Hetty. 'In your encyclopaedias.'

Hetty studied the kittens curled up together in their basket of rushes. There were at least twenty but they all looked exactly the same to her, black and sleek and sleepy-eyed. Then she spotted a tiny one all alone in a corner of the cave.

'I'll have that one,' she said decisively.

'Of course you can't!' hooted the witches.

'Why not?' demanded Hetty.

'You're just being silly,' said Thora.

'She's having you on,' said Cicely.

'A witch with a ginger cat! Whatever next?' tittered Celery.

'I want it,' said Hetty stubbornly. She burst into loud sobs and wouldn't be consoled. Eventually they agreed to let her have him; and if she wasn't up to scratch, she could take a black one as well.

The kitten was the same colour as Hetty's hair. Everyone remarked on the resemblance and everyone fell over him too, so Hetty decided to call him Trip-You-Up. She sat on a cushion and stroked his fur while the witches slurped tea and prattled on about what they'd seen in the crystal, the dreadful cost of vanishing cream and the pros and cons of a non-stick-cauldron. After half an hour, even Trip-You-Up seemed bored. He blinked at Hetty, then yawned and stretched, and finally strolled away. He really was very sweet, she thought to herself, even if he wasn't a dog. So when she saw him disappear into a narrow tunnel at the back of the cave, she wriggled in after him.

It was a bit of a squeeze for a Growing Girl. At one point Hetty was completely stuck, like a maggot in an apple, but after much huffing and puffing and worming and squirming she managed to work herself free. She slithered along in the darkness, feeling her way in case there was a fallen rock or a dangerous drop. If only she had thought to bring her glow-worms! But they were tucked up snug and warm in her cloak pocket, hanging on a hook at the witches' cave. She was beginning to wonder whether the tunnel would ever come to an end when she rounded a corner and saw daylight.

The tunnel opened out into a smooth, airy cave. Hetty dusted herself down and glanced about her. There didn't seem to be any bears or dragons and as she was feeling brave she was a little disappointed. Then she noticed some strange markings on the wall and when she went to take a closer look she realized they were paintings. There were pigs and fish and fabulous beasts, curious birds and furious bees, and not one bear but a whole family of them. Hetty was sure she had seen the pictures before, in Thora's encyclopaedia, in the chapter about 'Our Amazing Ancestors'. She would have to look it up when she got home but first of all she had to find Trip-You-Up.

The kitten was sitting at the mouth of the cave washing his paws. Poor Hetty took one look outside and had to cling to a rock to steady herself. They were on a ledge by a waterfall, near the top of a ravine. Although it was only about six broomsticks across it was so deep that Hetty nearly fainted. She was plucking up the courage to take another step when she heard a shout. On the other side of the ravine, behind a fence, was a little girl. She waved

and after a moment's hesitation Hetty waved back. She had never seen another child before, so you can imagine her surprise when a *second* child appeared, then another, and another, until there were no less than twenty-nine little girls smiling and waving at her from behind the fence. (At first Hetty thought they were fairies, but they were far too noisy and didn't have wings.) They all wore exactly the same clothes: red-and-white stripy dresses with clean white collars and a line of buttons down the front. Hetty thought they were the loveliest clothes she had ever seen.

The first girl shouted, 'Why are you dressed up as a witch?'

'I *am* a witch,' replied Hetty, wishing she wasn't. She felt so ashamed of her shabby black dress. The children nudged one another and giggled.

'I don't believe in witches,' shouted a girl with a ponytail.

'Me neither!' yelled the others.

After a while the children began to lose interest. One by one they wandered off and Hetty watched enviously as they played together in the sunshine. Some had skipping-ropes, others had kites, a few played bat and ball, while the rest took it in turn to ride bicycles. Two fat ladies had dogs on strings, just like the one in Thora's encyclopaedia.

For the first time in her life Hetty felt desperately lonely. She hadn't anyone to play with except Auld Frowstie and he didn't really count. She longed to join the children on the other side but the only way across would be by broomstick and the very thought of it made her feel queasy. A raindrop landed on her nose, then all of a sudden there was a downpour, a rainbow spread over the ravine, and a fat lady blew a whistle. The children scurried into a long green hut which had ICES painted in huge letters on the roof. For a few minutes Hetty waited, hoping that they would come out again, but she was disappointed.

The witches were dressed up in their cloaks and hats all ready to leave when Hetty reappeared.

'Where have you been? You're soaking!' they shrieked.

'Your best dress!' howled Sibyl.

'What have you been doing, child? Speak up!' commanded Thora.

Excitedly Hetty told them about the tunnel and the stripy children and the woman with the whistle.

'You must have seen a school party!' chuckled Emmerly, ruffling Hetty's hair. 'We used to see them in our day, didn't we, dear?'

A School Party. So that was it! 'I'd like to go to a School Party,' said Hetty. 'Do you have to have an invitation?'

'You'd have to go to school first!' laughed Emmerly, and Thora gave her such a dreadful look she quickly changed the subject.

'I know where you've been, Hetty,' she said. 'We used to play in that cave when we were little. It comes out by the Falls of Lostbuttie. Did you see our paintings?'

When the witches reached home, Hetty had a bowl of broth and went to bed early. She was tired but she could never remember feeling so happy. For a long time she lay awake, imagining herself in a stripy dress dancing beneath the rainbow with the other children. The other side of the waterfall looked much more interesting than the Blasted Heath. If only there was a way across? She couldn't wait to go to the Cave of Moistbleb for tea again, even if it did smell, and the chance to go down the tunnel was worth every mouthful of Emmerly's squash.

Sybil and Thora sat in the kitchen, talking in worried whispers.

'I don't like it,' said Thora. 'If she gets a taste for the Other Side she could fly away, and we might never see her again.'

'Fly? Hetty? She wouldn't dare!' said Sibyl. Then she added sadly, 'We've done our best to protect her but she asked me what a bicycle was the other day. Goodness knows where she learned such a word! I didn't know where to look.'

'If she goes, the power goes with her. And if she gets stung by a nettle it will be lost for ever,' said Thora. 'She *has* to stay. We *need* her. I'll lock the flying ointment in the wand cabinet, just in case. And you'd better bury those encyclopaedias the minute you've done the washing up.'

8

The Proficiency Test

If there was one thing more than any other that Hetty hated about being a witch, it was the meetings. Twice a month, ever since she was five, she had been bundled onto the back of a broomstick and flown to the Mountain Rescue Hut. She wasn't sure which was worse: being stuck behind Sibyl as she dithered about, stopping and starting, tilting and wobbling, wondering why she was losing height; or behind Thora, who flew in a straight line at high speed, bellowing at anything that got in her way. Hetty was always relieved when they reached the Mountain Rescue Hut. Climbers didn't use it because it was rather haunted, but the Blasted Heath Branch of the Witches' Institute found it very comfortable. They met there on the stroke of midnight, to swap spells and gossip and spooky stories.

The witches were always delighted to see Hetty. They made her call them 'Auntie' this and 'Auntie' that, and as soon as they set eyes on her they would exclaim, 'My word, haven't you grown!' 'What a big girl!' One after another they would prod Hetty to see how plump she was, or peer into her mouth to count her teeth; then Sybil would say, 'Recite your poem, Hetty, show them what a clever girl you are!' Hetty would mutter it under her breath; and when she had finished the ladies would clap their hands and cuddle her, and give her sticky sweets with fillings inside them (not nice ones, like strawberry cream or chocolate fudge, but the hard sort that you get at the dentist).

Hetty wasn't actually a member of the Witches' Institute, because there were only thirteen* places and (fortunately for her) they were all taken. So she was allowed to stay in the cloakroom and play with the cats till she fell asleep. Sometimes Hetty would creep into a corner and watch the witches but they got up to such silly things she was always sent out for giggling. The meetings began when Thora called the register. That was followed by Fingernail Inspection and Foot Inspection, then Notices and Maze-Dance practice. After a break for tea and biscuits there was a competition (at New Moon) or a ghost speaker (at Full Moon). At the end of the

* *Witches consider the number fourteen to be most unlucky.*

The Witches' Institute
(Blasted Heath Branch)

Chairwoman: **Thora Weird**...A Highly Scientific witch
Hon. Sec.: **Sibyl Weird**...A skilled herbalist, and
Thora's younger sister

MEMBERS

Audrey...A freshwater fisherwoman (deliveries Friday)
Ivy...A hatter. Also part-time caretaker at the
Mountain Rescue Hut (Headquarters of the W.I.)
Emmerly and Esmé...Elderly sisters who breed cats
and weave baskets.
Cicely...A maker of rushlights, candles and nasty soap
Celery...A shepherd: supplier of fleece and fine haggis
Hilary...A turf-cutter and bird-catcher
Hebony...Local agent for SPELL (Sorcery Products
and Equipment of Lancashire Ltd)
Penelope and Persephone...Twins (not identical).
Woodcutters and charcoal burners who live in
Birnam Wood.
Young Telephone...(Pronounced like Penelope). A
bespoke broomstick maker. Also does repairs and
servicing.

night the Witches played the Ride of the Valkyrie on combs and paper, and then it was time to go home.

One day, soon after Hetty's seventh birthday, Thora received a letter. She read it twice, then stared thoughtfully at the little girl.

'You will be sorry to hear that Hebony is leaving the Witches' Institute. She is moving to Lancashire, to live with her sister. That means we have a vacancy, and I propose you should take her place. What do you say to that?'

'I'm much too young and it's very bad for me to stay up so late,' said Hetty promptly.

'That's settled then,' beamed Thora. 'You can start next month.'

Hetty was furious. 'I don't want to join your rotten old club! I'm a mere child, at least that's what you're always telling me!'

'That's quite enough!' snapped the witch. 'In years to come when you are chairwoman of the W.I. you will look back and thank me.'

A few days later Hetty had a nice surprise. There were three brown-paper parcels beside her plate at breakfast-time.

'Yes, they're for you,' said Thora, and she smiled so nicely that Hetty felt all muddled up.

The first parcel was round and heavy and Hetty guessed at once it was a crystal ball. She thought the long thin one would be a wand, but it turned out to be a special stick for stirring potions. The last parcel was a book, *The Illustrated Junior Spelling Dictionary*.

Hetty was looking at the pictures of poisonous plants when Thora dropped her bombshell.

'Now that you have the equipment you must learn how to use it,' she told her. 'Come to my workshop at nine o'clock sharp. And during lessons you are to call me Miss Weird.'

Hetty's lessons were not a success. Truth to tell, she was bored and would far rather have helped Sybil in the kitchen than learn long passages from the Witches' Almanack. But Thora's mind was made up. Hetty would be the youngest witch ever to pass the Witches' Institute's Basic Proficiency Test. Every morning at two minutes past nine Thora unlocked the wand cabinet and took out two wands – an ebony one for herself, and an ivory one for Hetty.

'Hold your wand in the First Position and say "Hocus Pocus",' she commanded. 'And for goodness' sake, look mysterious.'

'Hocus Pocus,' muttered Hetty sullenly.

'*No! No! No!* Put a bit of enthusiasm into it girl!' screamed Thora. 'Now try again.'

Hetty glowered and said nothing.

'I'm waiting,' said Thora in an icy voice.

Hetty slumped right down in her seat and gazed at a rusty hook in the wall, determined to be as unmagical as she possibly could. But the hook began to wiggle and jiggle, and fell with a clang onto her notebook, bringing a lump of plaster with it.

'It's not fair!' Hetty complained to Sybil when she came in for lunch. 'I never asked to be a witch. Why should I do her smelly old spells? Why do I have to wear nettle-proof socks, and horrible scratchy black clothes?'

Sybil sighed and put down her turnip. 'Oh Hetty, why are you so stubborn? Lessons *are* boring, but we all have to do them. You'll never get your wand if you carry on like this.'

'What wand?' demanded Hetty, and Sybil looked guilty.

'Oh dear, perhaps I shouldn't have mentioned it. Thora's going to give you her second-best one when you've passed the Proficiency Test.'

Hetty's eyes lit up. A wand of her own? Imagine what she could do with that! She could try for a stripy dress, a black and white dog, or even a bicycle.

From then on Hetty was up before daybreak. She didn't dawdle over breakfast or pretend she was poorly; she rushed straight to the workshop to practise. Thora gaped in astonishment as she did her wandwork exercises, chanting spells, or reciting rules from the Witches' Almanack. In less than a week she learned to whip up a mist in a mixing bowl and cure a wart with a piece of string. She copied out the Cauldron Safety Code, and when she knew it by heart, Thora let her do Basic Wet Spell No. 1 (which made an awful mess of the ceiling) and Basic Wet Spell No.2 (which made treacle toffee). After that they studied Dry Spells. They were easier, and safer, too, because you didn't need anything except words and a wand. Hetty turned out to be exceptionally good at them, and by the end of a month Thora decided she was ready to take her test.

On the night of the full moon Hetty was filled with dread. She didn't utter a word until she and Thora reached the Mountain Rescue Hut and then she asked,

'Do I have to do my spell in front of everyone?'

'Indeed you do,' replied Thora, pushing her inside.

When Thora had called the register it was time for the test. 'Good luck!' hissed the witches, as Hetty stepped into the magic circle.

Thora held out her second-best wand and said,

'Hecate Weird, using this wand, and any other equipment necessary, you are to prepare and perform the spell of your choice. Marks will be awarded out of ten. You have thirty minutes, start-ing...*now!*'

Hetty no longer looked worried, in fact, she seemed quite confident. She pulled off her new woolly jumper (Sibyl had knitted it specially for the occasion) and spread it flat in the middle of the ring. Then she placed a kipper on the jumper and sat Trip-You-Up beside it. He snuffled about for a few minutes and when he was comfortable Hetty bowed politely and said,

'Good evening, Madam Chairwoman and Members of the Witches' Institute. Tonight I am going to perform a dry spell that I made up myself. In a few minutes you will see my jumper change colour from bat black to true blue.'

'What?' spluttered Thora. They hadn't practised this. Hetty was supposed to be waterproofing her cloak. What was the wretched girl thinking of? Everyone moved a little closer and watched with interest as Hetty marched slowly round the ring chanting,

> *'Hurlo-thrumbo*
> *Mumbo jumbo*
> *Hocus pocus*
> *Humble bum bee;*
> *Higgledy piggledy*
> *Jiggery pokery*
> *Hysteron proteron*
> *Marrowfat pea.'*

Then she stopped, spun round, and pointed her wand at the jumper. Everyone held their breath. After a few minutes somebody said, 'What an extraordinary spell!' and Sibyl whispered, 'Perhaps you'd better try once more, dear.' Hetty tried three times and was about to start again when Thora pointed to the sand-glass and said grimly,

'Time's up. I'm afraid you've failed, Hecate.'

Hetty threw down the wand and burst into tears. She had set her heart on keeping it.

'Poor little mite! She's tried so hard,' said the witches and some of them began to cry too. They begged Thora to let Hetty pass but she refused.

'It's against the rules,' she said firmly.

The next day Hetty was miserable. She couldn't think what had gone wrong with her spell. It had worked on the dishcloth and the net thing the onions were kept in. Sybil was all weepy and Thora was angry. 'You should have stuck to something simple,' she scolded. 'You have disgraced me in front of the entire Witches' Institute!'

'Do let's change the subject,' begged Sibyl. To her relief there was a knock at the door and Audrey burst in.

'Guess what?' she said excitedly. 'Celery's sheep have died.'

'All of them?' asked Thora and Audrey nodded.

'How dreadful!' exclaimed Sibyl. 'Was it something they ate?'

'No, no!' cried Audrey impatiently. 'They haven't died. They've dyed! Now we can all have blue jumpers! You *are* a clever girl, Hetty!'

Hetty was enrolled at the New Moon meeting in March and as it was a special occasion the Witches performed the Friendship Ceremony in her honour. They skipped solemnly round her, stopping at intervals to clatter their broomsticks together. Then they sat in a circle and pulled off their socks. 'Abracadabra!' they chorused and each witch presented her right sock to the lady on her left. 'Abracadabra!' they said again and passed their left socks to the lady on the right. Then they put them on and Hetty tried hard not to giggle, because everyone was wearing their very best cloaks and odd socks. Then, with a great trumpeting, the witches blew their noses and put their handkerchiefs into Thora's hat, ready for the lucky dip.

Later that night Thora gave Hetty her wand, together with a shiny hat-badge and an important certificate with her name on. In return Hetty promised never to do any wicked spells, or put curses on people.

'Welcome to the Witches' Institute!' everyone cried, shaking Hetty by the hand. 'A real witch at last!'

'What are you going to do, now you've got your wand?' they wanted to know. 'Have you decided yet?'

'First spells are so thrilling,' said Emmerly wistfully.

'It's not nearly such fun when you're older,' agreed Esmé.

Hetty smiled at them sweetly. She knew *exactly* what she was going to do.

9
Enter Macbeth

Hetty didn't trust the witches and was afraid to let her wand out of sight. Instead of locking it in the cabinet with the others she kept it in her pocket until bedtime, when she tucked it under her pillow for safety. Curiously, it seemed to make her dream. Her favourite dream was of a sunny room that was almost square. Its walls were dotted with little yellow flowers and there were primrose curtains to match. In one corner there was a bed: a *clean* bed, with a patchwork quilt and crisp white pillowcases. One day at breakfast she told Sibyl about it, but the witch didn't seem interested.

'Must have been the cheese at supper,' she said gruffly. 'If you ate the maggots and left the cheese like everyone else, you wouldn't have bad dreams.'

'It wasn't a bad dream,' sighed Hetty. 'It was lovely. Really lovely.'

Since Hebony had left to live in Lancashire her tiny cottage had fallen into ruin. Thistles poked up through the thatch, creeper covered the windows, and brambles blocked the cobbled path. Vegetables rotted in the ground, while the nettle patch spread and set seed. Some of the seeds reached Bogwater Cottage where they sprouted unseen in the soft dark soil. One warm summer night Sibyl got stung, pulling up a turnip. Immediately her sister declared a State of Emergency and Hetty was locked indoors until further notice.

One morning while the witches were out looking for nettles, Hetty had an idea. She fetched a broom and swept the bedroom, then paid Auld Frowstie two biscuits to suck up the fluff and one more for blowing away the cobwebs. Then she scrubbed the walls and began to scrape the bat-droppings off the furniture. In the afternoon she cleaned the windows (only the insides, of course, because she wasn't allowed out) and washed the curtains in the cauldron. They turned out to be yellow: a very deep yellow like the yolk of an egg. While they were drying Hetty painted some flower pictures and pinned them on the wall. By the time the witches came in for supper the bedroom looked almost as nice as the one in her dream.

Hetty knew they wouldn't be pleased with her, but she hadn't expected them to be quite so cross. Even Sybil was nasty.

'You're downright peculiar, there's no two ways about it,' she shouted when she saw what Hetty had done. 'It takes years to grow mushrooms on a mattress! It'll never be the same again!'

Hetty said she was sorry but she didn't mean it. 'That does it,' she thought to herself. 'I'm off! And when I'm gone they'll be *really* sorry!'

The next day, as soon as the witches had left the cottage, Hetty searched through Thora's spell books. There seemed to be a spell for almost everything except for what Hetty wanted. *The Cauldron Bleu Encyclopaedia* was six inches thick but the word 'School' wasn't even in the index. She looked under 'Party' but that wasn't mentioned either. She was about to give up when a piece of paper fluttered to the floor. It was old and yellowed and burnt around the edge.

The spell was perfect. Hetty fetched a sheet of paper and wrote:

Pumpkin seeds   Slugs
Aconite   Cockroaches
Ragwort   Hemlock
Toadstools   Owl pellets
Yew   Owl pellets
                   Leeches

Are you bored? Lonely? Unhappy with your life? Then why not try a change-of-scene spell? It's as easy as ABC!

Using the initial letters from the table below, spell the name of your desired destination and gather the ingredients accordingly. For example, if you wish to visit a) Dublin or b) Hexham, you will require:

Deadly nightshade, **U**nderwear, **B**atfood, **L**eeches, **I**ron filings, **N**ewts, **H**emlock, **E**arwigs, **X**tra-strong mince, **H**emlock, **A**conite, **M**ink

TABLE OF CONTENTS

Aconite (monkshood), 6 stems
Batfood, 4 scoops
Cockroaches, 2 shelled
Deadly nightshade, 7 sprigs
Earwigs, 3 heaped tablespoons
Frogspawn, 2 handfuls
Gunpowder, 1 bucketful
Hemlock, 30 leaves
Iron filings, 6 tablespoons
Jackdaw (plucked)
Kippers, 4 (not fillets)
Leeches, 1 dozen
Mink (semi-skinned)

Newts, 13 (unsalted)
Owl pellets, 6
Pumpkin seeds, 7 cupfuls
Quicksilver, 3 teaspoons
Ragworm, 1 hatful, finely chopped
Slugs, 70 (orange are best)
Toadstools (fresh or dried), 2 dozen
Underwear, 3 items (never washed)
Viper (medium sliced)
Worms, 1 packet (Teatime Assortment)
Xtra-strong mince, 1 bootful
Yew leaves (generous bunch)
Zinc ointment, 1 large jar

METHOD

Place 3 gallons of bogwater in a cauldron and bring briskly to the boil. Add a bouquet ghastly, then cast in the ingredients, one at a time, in the correct order of spelling. Perform Wand-Dance 9 (Highland Version). Add plenty of yeast, season well, and leave to ferment for five days or longer, stirring occasionally.

N.B. The stirring should be done by another person.

Then she crept into the larder and reached down a jar of leeches, a sack of pumpkin seeds, and a string of dried toadstools. Hetty had a talent for finding things. (Sibyl always said she could find a mouse in a cattery if she put her mind to it.) She rummaged about and discovered two fat cockroaches, one in the cake-tin, and another in the teapot.

After lunch Thora decided it was safe for Hetty to go out – but not until she had put on two thick pairs of nettle-proof socks and gloves. Hetty wandered slowly round the garden, pausing now and then to pick up a slug or an owl pellet with a tiny pair of tongs.

When Sibyl wasn't looking she borrowed her magic scythe and cut a bunch of flowers from the Poisonous Border. There was a yew tree growing at the far end, neatly clipped in the shape of a crow. Hetty snipped off his tail feathers and hurried round to the back of Thora's workshop. The Little Witch's Cauldron had begun to boil. All she needed now was Another Person.

'I need your help,' she told Auld Frowstie. 'I want to do a spell but I can't manage it on my own.'

'What sort of spell?' he asked suspiciously, but when he heard it was a Going-Away spell he agreed at once to help her. 'How soooooon are you going?' he wailed.

'As soon as I can,' said Hetty earnestly. 'I want to go to school and have fun and games and a stripy dress, just like other children.'

'You *want* to go to school?' he howled. 'Yooooo give me the creeeeps!'

The next morning, and every morning after that, Hetty and Auld Frowstie went to inspect the potion. It always looked exactly the same: green and watery with a few nasty-looking bits floating on the surface. But on the seventh day it had changed colour.

'I think something's happening,' cried Hetty excitedly, handing Auld Frowstie a stick. But as she watched him stir the mixture she began to feel sad. She pulled the rim of her hat right down and hoped he wouldn't see her tears.

'It's time we said goodbye,' she said quietly. 'Thank you for helping me. We probably won't see one another ever again. But I'll often think of you.' She did her best to hug him but he was too wispy.

All of a sudden there was a disgusting fishy smell and thick foam, the colour of raspberries, came frothing out of the cauldron and onto the grass. Trip-You-Up (who had been half-asleep on top of the wood-pile) arched his back and hissed angrily.

'Oooooooh, yoooo've done it now, Hetty!' wailed the ghost. 'Wait till Thora sees that!'

'Don't fuss. It'll stop in a minute,' said Hetty, but the froth just kept on coming. She fumbled for her wand, but it wasn't in her pocket. It must have dropped out when she tried to hug Auld Frowstie. In

89

desperation she fell to her knees and scrabbled in the foam.

'*Hecate Weird, what are you up to?*'

Hetty nearly jumped out of her skin. To her relief the voice wasn't Thora's, it was Young Telephone's. She was Highly Magical, everybody said so. She'd know what to do.

'*Ragwort?*' repeated the witch, when Hetty told her what she had put in the potion. 'You used ragwort? No one *ever* uses ragwort, it's far too strong. Any idiot could tell you that.'

'That's what it says in my recipe,' said Hetty indignantly. She pulled a rumpled piece of paper from her pocket and showed it to Young Telephone.

'My word, Hecate, you have been careless!' exclaimed the witch.

'That last letter's M, not T! It's *Ragworm*, not *ragwort!*'

At that moment Sibyl was bent over her vegetable patch talking to a cabbage.

'I'm so sorry,' she said. 'You know I'd sooner leave you snug and warm in your cosy bed, but we shall have to eat something and I promise I'll pull you up as gently as...'

'Pardon me for interrupting,' said the cabbage and Sybil froze. She opened her mouth to call for Thora but only a squeak came out.

'I do apologize for disturbing you,' continued the cabbage in a deep voice. 'But I appear to be lost.'

A cabbage? Lost? That couldn't be right. Sybil

90

straightened up and found herself face to face with a man in muddy suit. He was carrying an umbrella and a smart black briefcase.

'I wonder if you would be so kind as to direct me to the Town Hall?' he asked politely.

'What Town Hall?' said Sibyl blankly.

The man looked confused. 'I do feel peculiar,' he said. 'And my head aches.'

'What you need is a nice hot cup of tea,' said Sybil kindly. 'Come into my cottage and I'll put the cauldron on.'

While Sybil was busy in the kitchen the man leaned back in Thora's chair and wondered how on earth he came to be in such a place. He was still wondering when a flowery cup and saucer floated towards him and landed with a chink on a little round table. They were followed by a very old cake, all covered in dust, and then a sugar basin.

'One lump or twoooooooooo?' said a voice in his ear. The man looked round but there was nobody there. He felt his forehead, then checked his pulse; it must be time for one of his pills. But when he opened his briefcase his pills had gone. And so had his diary, his papers, his calculator, his mobile telephone, and even his cheese-and-tomato sandwiches. There was nothing in his briefcase except for a big brown envelope. He was frowning at it when Thora came in.

'Do you happen to know this address?' he asked nervously.

'Of course I do!' she snapped. 'I'll have that if you don't mind. It's addressed to me!'

The envelope was full of official-looking forms and papers, together with some maps and plans and a letter marked EXTREMELY URGENT. Thora read it aloud.

··I DINNA KEN··

Glasburgh City Council
Housing Division
Director of Housing: R. Halesome

Burns House
Pylon Road
Glasburgh
GB1 1AE
Tel: 01324 78432
Fax: 01324 78392

Our ref: DM/6829481
22nd July 1996

Dear Misses Weird,

I have been instructed by the Department of Environment and the Caledonian Water Company to inform you that the Blasted Heath is to be flooded to form a reservoir. Your cottage has been compulsorily purchased, and I have arranged accommodation for you on the Living- stone Estate in the Dunisdane district of Glasburgh. Please be ready to move by July 31st. (Note that your new accommodation is to be furnished to a high standard, and only a limited amount of personal property can be transported. In the meantime, I will be happy to assist you in completing the enclosed forms.

I trust this will not inconvenience you,
Yours faithfully

Dale Macbeth, District Housing Officer

'This, I presume, is *your* signature?' snarled Thora, waving the letter under the visitor's nose.

'It is indeed,' agreed Dale Macbeth, looking bewildered. 'I can't understand it! I know about the reservoir, but I didn't know anything about *you*! And I *certainly* don't remember typing this letter.'

Sibyl began to cry. 'Our lovely cottage!' she sobbed. 'All under water! I can't bear to think about it!'

Mr Macbeth felt embarrassed. 'I'm sure you'll find your new home extremely comfortable. Dunsinane's a nice part of town, very handy for the shops and buses. And the schools are excellent,' he added, glancing at Hetty who had been watching from the doorway.

School? He said *school*! So the spell *had* worked, after all. Hetty wanted to shout *hooray* and dance round the room but she thought it best to keep quiet.

Sibyl was no longer tearful, she was angry. 'Why *should* we go?' she shrieked. 'Our family has lived here for thirteen generations. What about the garden? And my goats? Where can we keep the chickens? And I insist on having my own well. I'm not moving unless...'

Thora glared at her.

'There's only one thing we need to know,' she said slowly, fixing her gaze on the visitor. 'Tell me, Mr Macbeth: are there – or are there not – stinging nettles in Glasburgh?'

Mr Macbeth seemed surprised at the question. 'I've never seen any,' he admitted. 'But I'm sure we could arrange…'

'That's settled then!' said Thora. 'We move on the thirty-first!'

10
Moving Day

We move on the thirty-first.' The words went round and round in Hetty's head. In a few days' time she would be at school! She would have a stripy dress, and friends to play with, maybe even a bicycle. It was a pity Sibyl and Thora were coming too. How like them to spoil things! Hetty remembered seeing grown-ups with the school party and supposed they must be witches, although they hadn't been wearing hats. She was still wondering when the Witches' Institute burst in.

'We saw a stranger in the crystal,' cried Audrey.

'He had a beard.'

'And a briefcase.'

'Look! There he is!' shrieked Persephone. 'In the chair!'

The witches clustered round to take a look at Mr Macbeth, who gave a funny little moan and shrank further into his seat.

'He does look strange,' remarked Penelope.

'I *feel* strange,' groaned Mr Macbeth.

To their disappointment he didn't say anything after that. Sibyl started to tell the witches what happened in the cabbage patch but Thora interrupted. The reservoir was much more interesting, she insisted. The witches were amazed when they heard the news. Would there be fish, they wanted to know. How many kinds? Would residents be given boats? They were all talking and arguing so noisily that no one noticed Mr Macbeth was getting fainter. By the end of the evening he had completely disappeared, leaving nothing but his big brown envelope.

There was a great deal to be done before the thirty-first. Bogwater Cottage had been standing for over four hundred years, and in all that time no one had ever thrown anything away. The next day Sibyl and Hetty were up till midnight, emptying the cupboards and turning out the sheds. They piled everything in a heap by the newt-pond and gazed at it.

'What do we do now?' asked Hetty.

'Easy!' said Sibyl. 'We'll find the Most Important Thing and the rest can go on the bonfire.'

They arranged the rubbish in a circle: potions that had dried up, or had their labels missing, old boots, odd bones, cracked bottles, chipped crystals, bent cauldrons, mouldy blankets and broken broomsticks. Sybil pulled on her hat and called, 'Stand back, Hetty, dear! I'm about to twirl!' Round she went, faster and faster, until she finally lost her balance and tumbled over.

'That's decided, then!' she beamed, when she saw where her hat was pointing. 'We keep the blankets! You never know when they might come in useful.'

Sibyl's next task was to find homes for the animals. Thora had eaten the piglets (except one and he was coming to Dunsinane with the cats). Ivy wanted the goats, and although Audrey had agreed to take the things that flew she didn't need another owl and she certainly couldn't be trusted with a bat. The wild animals were even more of a worry. Sibyl prowled about the garden with a big black sack, dropping in rats, mice, weasels, hedgehogs, and anything else that happened to squeak. Then she flew up to Hebony's garden and set them free. On the last morning she made a raft out of rushes (in case anyone was left behind) and paid Auld Frowstie to tie it to the roof. He had just finished when Owl awoke and began to hoot.

Below, in the kitchen, the witches were having breakfast. 'Don't tease Owl, Hecate,' scolded Thora. 'It's extremely childish.'

'I'm not!' Hetty protested. 'It's that noise that's upsetting him.'

The witches stopped munching their stoat and listened. Hetty was right. There was a noise and it was getting louder all the time. The china on the dresser began to rattle, then the entire cottage seemed to shake.

'It's an earthquake! There's going to be an earthquake!' screamed Sibyl.

'Pull yourself together, woman!' snapped her sister. 'If you had been paying attention during my talk on local geology you would know that…'

'It's a giant!' cried Sibyl, and dived under the table.

'Whatever it is, I shall command it to go away,'

yelled Thora. 'Pass my wand, Hecate! The big one with the ebony handle.'

Thora marched outside and after a moment's hesitation Hetty followed.

'Shoo! Shoo! Abracadabra! Go away, you noisy brute!' the witch roared, flapping her cloak at a monstrous blue thing that was hovering overheard. The Thing ignored her and landed at the end of the garden, right in front of her workshop. Thora was furious. How *dare* it disobey her! Summoning all her courage she rushed forward and began to beat the Thing with her wand. Instantly a door opened and out jumped three men in matching T-shirts. One of them was shouting and making magic signs.

'*What's he saying?*' bellowed Thora. '*I can't hear a word.*'

'He says "*Any chance of a cup of tea, luv?*"' Hetty shouted back.

When the noise had stopped the men introduced themselves. Their names were Rocky, Cliff and Glenn, and they worked for Sky Blue Removals Ltd.

'Chap from the Council sent us,' said Cliff.

'To pack up your stuff,' added Glenn.

'Do you mean Mr Macbeth?' asked Sybil.

'That's the bloke!' said Rocky. 'He said to send his regards, and he'll meet you at the heliport. Where do you want us to start, missus? Lounge? Dining area? Master bedroom?'

'You can start with my workshop,' said Thora.

'This way, gentlemen.'

As soon as she unlocked the door the removal men began to cough.

'Gunpowder! You'll get used to it,' said Thora brusquely. 'Here – have a candle.'

'Gordon Bennett!' exclaimed Rocky. 'Did you ever see the like!'

The three men stared in astonishment at the maze of thin glass pipes and round-bottomed bottles filled with a slimy, spluttery, bubbly liquid. Around the walls were neat rows of jars and and test tubes, all arranged in strict alphabetical order. Glenn shuddered as he read the labels. Toad…Toadstools…Toad Stools…Toad Spawn…Toenails (mine)…Toenails (Sibyl's)…Toiletwater…Tonsils…

'I'm not sure that we're licensed to carry this lot,' said Cliff uneasily. 'We've moved some funny things in our time – we had to deliver a stuffed gorilla to an oil rig yesterday. And a grand piano to the Longstone lighthouse. But this…' He shook his head, quite lost for words.

At eight o'clock they were almost ready to leave. The very last tea-chest had been loaded into the helicopter and poor Sibyl was trying not to cry. 'Goodbye, cottage. Goodbye, garden. Goodbye, Bog. Goodbye, dear old crab apple,' she whispered sadly. She hugged the tree, and then kissed Audrey, Ivy, Emmerly, Esmé, Cicely, Celery, Hilary, Penelope, Persephone, and finally Young Telephone. (They had spotted the removal men in the crystal!)

101

Everyone was howling and sobbing, promising to write and keep in touch when Persephone screamed,

'*Look out!*'

They all had to duck as three broomsticks skimmed over the garden, and skidded to a halt beside the henhouse.

'Sting-a-ling! It's us!' trilled Rubella, poking Thora with the end of her broomstick. The Chairwoman of the Witches' Institute eyed it with distaste. It had curly handlebars that looked like horns, and on the front, where the cat-basket should have been, was a skull with a candle inside.

'What do you want?' she growled.

'Come to say ta-ta to the little boggart, haven't we?' grinned Smerelda.

'My, hasn't she grown since we last saw her?' sniggered Firkettle. 'How old are you now, dearie?'

'S-s-seven and a ha-half,' stammered Hetty nervously.

'S-s-seven and a ha-half!' echoed Smerelda. 'F-f-fancy that!' and they all cackled. Then they threw down their broomsticks and danced round Thora singing.

> '*Sting-a-ring o' rogueys,*
> *A pocket full of bogeys,*
> *We hissssss you! We hissssss you!*
> *And all bow down.*'

With that they whipped off their hats and bowed exaggeratedly.

'Greetings, your Majicksty,' smirked Rubella.

'We are your humble serpentsssssssssssss,' added Smerelda.

'At your servisssss!' finished Firkettle.

'That's quite enough!' said Thora, shaking with anger.

'We haven't sssssstarted yet,' they said gleefully.

Hetty was hiding behind Emmerly and Esmé. She gripped Young Telephone's hand. 'Who are they?' she asked in a frightened whisper.

'Never mind who they are, get into the helipocter,'

murmured the witch. 'Quick, while they're not looking!' She bundled Hetty up the steps and pushed her inside.

Glenn was about to strap Hetty into her seat when she cried, 'Trip-You-Up. I haven't got Trip-You-Up!'

Before Young Telephone could stop her she had run back down the steps, past the witches and into the Poisonous Border, where the cat liked to sleep among the leaves. Hetty stooped to pick him up, then she screamed.

The witches clustered round her, fussing and fretting, but Hetty was too upset to tell them what the matter was.

'Did you see a rat? A snake? A mink?' they shrieked. Hetty shook her head and pointed to her cheek. Eventually she managed to gasp, 'I've... been...stung!' and all the witches began to shout at once. Rubella, Smerelda and Firkettle were sobbing with laughter.

'Wotcher gonna do now, Weird? Find another baby?' spluttered Firkettle.

'Oooooo, what a shame!' sniggered her sisters, settling down on the compost heap to watch the fun. 'You've lost your pow-er! You've lost your pow-er!' they taunted, while the Witches' Institute ran in all directions, uprooting everything in search of the right sort of leaves.

Thora and Young Telephone were huddled together, talking urgently. After a moment Thora shouted, 'Gather round, ladies, chop-chop! Form a circle. We may be in time to save her.'

Sybil handed round dock-leaves, and when Young Telephone raised her wand the witches waved them about, singing,

> *'You put your dock-leaf in,*
> *Your dock-leaf out,*
> *In! Out! In! Out!*
> *Shake it all about;*
> *You do the Hokey-Pokey and you twirl around,*
> *That's how the spell comes out.'*

'Pathetic!' jeered Rubella.

'Rubbish!' sneered Smerelda.

'It'll never work!' crowed Firkettle. 'Admit it, Weird, the power's gone! Gone for ever.'

'We shall see,' said Thora grimly.

She took Hetty by the arm and marched her into the helicopter. Even though it was an emergency Thora still found time for a row with the removal men. 'Naturally I had assumed I would be driving,' she said coldly. 'I have more flying experience than the three of you put together. Come along, Sybil. We'll take the broomsticks.'

The removal men grinned at one another and shrugged. Rocky started the engines, the rotor blades began to spin, and within seconds they were in the air high above the heath and the waving witches.

When Hetty had stopped crying Glenn examined her swollen cheek. 'You don't need a dock-leaf!' he exclaimed. 'That's a bee-sting, unless I'm very much mistaken!' Hetty sat very still while he pulled it out with a pair of tweezers from the first-aid kit. Afterwards Glenn rubbed some ointment on her face, and gave her a toffee for being so brave. He started to tell her a story about a girl who ate some porridge that really belonged to some bears, but before he reached the end little Hetty was fast asleep.

Hetty awoke feeling cold. She was still moving, but she knew she wasn't in the helipocter because the noise had stopped. To her surprise she found herself squashed on a seat between Sibyl and Thora with a pair of antlers digging into her leg.

'Where am I?' she asked sleepily.

'You're in a taxi. Just coming into the City Centre,' said Mr Macbeth's voice. 'We'll be going over the bridge in a minute.'

Hetty sat up. Although it was night-time there were lights everywhere: orange, white, red, and green, lights that flashed and said CINEMA, CAFÉ BAR, PEKING CUISINE, PIZZA, BINGO, BALTI and KEBAB. The words meant nothing to her but they sounded mysterious, like the words of a spell.

Now they were going more slowly, past enormous windows that were filled with books, toys, shoes, saucepans, rugs, hats, beds, bicycles, and a hundred and one other things that Hetty didn't recognize. In one window people sat at tables, talking and eating buns out of little boxes. Another was full of children, still and staring, as though they were bewitched. They were identically dressed, except the boys were wearing trousers while the girls had skirts or tunics. They had stiff white shirts and stripy ties, and smart red jackets with badges on the pockets. Two children were holding up a banner that said

```
* BACK TO SKOOL *

* WINTER UNIFORM NOW IN STOCK *
```

and Hetty realized she had made a silly mistake. Skool was spelt with a K: She should have used kippers, not cockroaches and hemlock. Perhaps it wouldn't matter – it wasn't a very big mistake after all.

The windows came to an end and soon afterwards Mr Macbeth said, 'This is it, driver. You can drop us off here.' He turned and smiled at the witches.

'Welcome to Dunsinane, ladies! I hope you will be very happy!'

Sibyl sniffed and Thora said something I won't repeat, but Hetty was shivering with excitement. Her new life was about to begin.

Poor Hetty! She was so excited about starting school, but she would just have to be patient. It was the beginning of August and as everyone knows (except witches) nobody goes to school in the summer holidays.